Emily
the Emerald
Fairy

by Daisy Meadows

illustrated by Georgie Ripper

SCHOLASTIC INC.

New York   Toronto   London   Auckland   Sydney
Mexico City   New Delhi   Hong Kong   Buenos Aires

The
Fairyland
Palace

Adventure
Playground

Tippington
Manor

Tippington
Town

The Tall
Toy
Store

Fountain

By frosty magic I cast away
These seven jewels with their fiery rays,
So their magic powers will not be felt
And my icy castle shall not melt.

The fairies may search high and low
To find the gems and take them home.
But I will send my goblin guards
To make the fairies' mission hard.

Contents

Toy Trouble

"Wow!" Kirsty Tate gasped, her eyes wide with amazement. "This is the biggest toy store I've ever seen!"

Her best friend, Rachel Walker, laughed. "I know," she agreed. "Isn't it great?"

Kirsty nodded. Wherever she turned,

there was something wonderful to see. In one corner of the store was a huge display of dolls in every shape and size, along with an amazing number of dollhouses. A special roped-off area was filled with remote-control cars, buses, trucks, and airplanes. Nearby stood rows of bikes, skateboards, and scooters.

Shelves were piled high with every board game Kirsty could think of, plus

stacks of cool computer games. Colorful kites hung from the ceiling, along with big balloons and spinning mobiles. Kirsty had never seen anything like it, and this was only the first floor!

"Look over there, Kirsty," Rachel said, pointing at the dolls.

Kirsty saw a sign that read MEET FAIRY FLORENCE AND HER FRIENDS. She stared at the dolls displayed around the sign.

Fairy Florence wore a long pink dress. She looked boring and old-fashioned. Kirsty and Rachel glanced at each other and burst out laughing.

"Fairy Florence doesn't look like a real fairy at all!" Rachel whispered, and Kirsty nodded.

Rachel and Kirsty knew what real

fairies looked like because they'd met them . . . many times! The two girls had often visited Fairyland to help their fairy friends when they were in trouble. The problems were usually caused by icy Jack Frost. He was always making trouble with the help of his mean goblins.

Just a few days earlier, King Oberon and Queen Titania had asked Rachel and Kirsty to help them. Jack Frost had stolen the seven magic jewels from the queen's crown. The jewels were very important, because they controlled a lot of the magic in Fairyland.

Jack Frost had wanted the magic for himself, but after the heat and light of the jewels began to melt his ice castle, he had angrily thrown the gems far into the

human world. Now it was up to the girls to return the jewels to Fairyland, before the fairies' magic ran out for good.

"I hope we can find the rest of the magic jewels before I go home," Kirsty said to Rachel, looking worried. "After all, I'm only staying with you until the end of school break."

"Well, we found India's moonstone and Scarlett's garnet," Rachel reminded her. "We just have to keep our eyes open for the others."

"Yes, we have to watch out for goblins and magic jewels!" Kirsty said. The girls knew that Jack Frost had sent his goblins to find and guard the gems, so that the fairies wouldn't get them back.

"Here you are, girls," said Rachel's dad as he joined them. "Do you two want to look around the toy store on your own? We can meet up in a little while."

"Dad can't wait to check out the train section," Rachel told Kirsty with a grin. "It's his favorite part of the store."

Mr. Walker laughed. "Ah, but today I have the perfect excuse," he said. "I'm buying something for my godson, Mark.

It's his birthday soon, and he loves trains."

Toot, toot!

The sudden sound of a whistle made Kirsty jump.

"Watch out, Kirsty!" Rachel cried with a smile. "There's a train coming!"

Kirsty looked up. For the first time, she noticed that a train track ran around the store above their heads. It weaved its way in and out of the displays. A toy train was whizzing along the track toward them, blowing its whistle. "Isn't it fun?" Mr.

Walker asked, beaming as the train sped by. "I'll see you two later. Meet me at the front entrance in half an hour."

"OK," Rachel replied. She grinned at Kirsty. "Come on, let's take a look around."

The girls wandered past the dolls, and over to a roped-off area where customers were playing with remote-control cars.

"Aren't they fast?" Kirsty remarked, staring at a bright red car that was zooming back and forth across the floor.

"I think we should buy this red one," the woman next to Kirsty said, turning to her husband with a smile. "Stuart will love it!"

Her husband, who held the controls in his hand, pushed a button. The car skidded to a stop, then flipped over and landed on its wheels before zooming off again.

"That's cool!" Kirsty gasped, very impressed.

"Isn't it?" the woman agreed, giving the two girls a friendly smile. "Our little boy, Stuart, will really enjoy playing with it." She glanced at her husband, who was now making the car whiz around in circles. "If he gets a chance, that is!"

Rachel and Kirsty laughed. They were just about to walk away when, suddenly, Kirsty caught sight of something out of the corner of her eye. Something silvery and glittering . . .

Kirsty spun around. There was a tall mirror on the wall near her, and the surface of the glass was moving. It rippled and shimmered, just like a pool of water.

"Oh!" Kirsty gasped. "Rachel, look!"

Rachel stared at the shimmering surface of the mirror, and her eyes widened. "Is it magic?" she whispered.

As the girls watched in amazement, a reflection appeared in the glass. Rachel and Kirsty could see a small boy, about seven years old, playing with the same shiny red car from the store. The boy pushed a button on the remote control, smiling as he watched the toy. The little red car came whizzing straight toward the girls!

Rachel and Kirsty turned around quickly, ready to jump out of the way of the speeding car. But to their amazement, there was nothing there. The boy and his toy car had disappeared!

Mirror Magic

Both Kirsty and Rachel blinked hard and looked around the store. There were little boys nearby, but they didn't see the boy they had been watching in the mirror. How could he have disappeared so quickly?

"What just happened?" Rachel asked,

rubbing her eyes. "Were we seeing things?"

Kirsty turned back to the mirror again. The magical shimmer was gone now, and the glass looked completely flat and normal again. In the mirror, Kirsty saw the reflection of the man and woman who had been looking at the red car. Now they were paying for the toy at the counter behind her.

"But the boy looked so real," she said to Rachel.

"It must be fairy magic," Rachel whispered as they walked away. "But what does it mean?"

"I don't know," Kirsty replied. "Maybe we'll find out soon!"

The girls walked into another part of the store that was full of practical jokes and little toys. There were shelves full of rubber spiders, plastic soldiers, dinosaurs, farm animals, pencils, erasers, paints, and beads.

"Mom!" A little girl ran down the aisle toward Rachel and Kirsty. She looked  very excited, and was waving a large, plastic bottle of bubble mixture in her hand. "Mom, where are you? I want this one! It says it blows the biggest bubbles in the whole world!"

But as the little girl passed Rachel and Kirsty, the bottle slipped from her fingers. It crashed to the floor and cracked open. Frothy bubble mix spilled out.

"Oh!" the little girl gasped, and burst into tears.

"It's OK, don't cry," Kirsty said quickly. "It was an accident."

Just then, the little girl's mom hurried toward them, followed by a salesperson.

"Oh, Katie!" the woman said, giving her daughter a hug. "Don't worry, I'll buy you another one."

"And we'll get that cleaned up right away," said the salesclerk kindly.

"Thank you so much," Katie's mom said gratefully.

Smiling now, the little girl and her mom walked off to find another bottle of bubbles, while the salesperson went to get a mop.

"Should we go look at the dollhouses?" Kirsty suggested.

But Rachel was staring at the floor in amazement. "Kirsty, look at that!" she whispered, clutching her friend's arm.

Kirsty looked down. The pool of bubble mixture was shimmering and

rippling on the floor, just like the mirror! Slowly, the girls saw a picture form in the liquid. It was Katie. She seemed to be playing happily in a sunny garden, blowing big, beautiful bubbles.

"This *has* to be fairy magic," Rachel said as the picture faded. "I think we're seeing things that are going to happen in the future! We saw Katie playing with her bubbles at home, and the little boy with the red car must have been Stuart."

Kirsty looked thoughtful. "Do you think the magic emerald could be nearby?" she asked. "That's the jewel that controls seeing magic."

Rachel nodded. "I think you're right —" she began.

Toot, toot!

The girls glanced up to see the store's little train chugging along its track, just above their heads.

But as it came closer, Rachel stared.

"There's something sparkly in the first car of the train," she pointed out.

Kirsty peered hard at the train and suddenly realized what Rachel had seen. "It's Emily the Emerald Fairy!" she gasped happily.

A Goblin Drops By

Emily was leaning out of the train and waving her sparkly, emerald-green wand at Rachel and Kirsty. As the train came closer to the girls, Emily fluttered out and landed on Rachel's shoulder. She wore a short green dress and ballet slippers in exactly the same color. Long, shiny red hair tumbled down her back. It was held

away from her face by a dazzling
emerald clip in the shape of a dragonfly.

"At last!" Emily beamed, her green
eyes sparkling. "I'm so happy to see you.
I've been looking for you everywhere!"

"And we're happy to see you," Kirsty
replied. "Some really strange things have
been happening around here."

"Let's go over behind that display

rack," said Rachel quickly, looking around to make sure that nobody was watching them. "We have lots to tell you, Emily!"

When they were safely hidden from the other customers, the girls told Emily about the pictures they'd seen in the mirror and the bubble mixture.

Emily nodded.

"That's seeing magic," she told them. "It means my emerald is nearby."

"We'll help you look for it," said Kirsty.

"But there are lots of places it could

27

be," Rachel added, frowning as she looked around the enormous store.

"And there are lots of places for goblins to hide, too," Emily pointed out. She fluttered down and slipped into Rachel's pocket. "We need to be careful."

The two girls walked into the middle of the store and began to wander through the aisles. Emily peeked out of Rachel's pocket.

Suddenly Rachel grabbed Kirsty's arm. "What's that green sparkle over there?" she asked excitedly.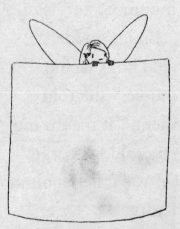

"Where?" Kirsty asked.

"In the doll section," Rachel replied, pointing. Her heart pounding, she led the way across the room to the glimmer of green she had seen. "I know it's around here somewhere."

"Was that it?" Kirsty asked, pointing at one of the dolls. It was wearing a necklace of shiny green beads that glittered in the light.

Rachel looked at the doll more closely, and her face fell. "Yes, I think it was," she said, sighing.

"Don't worry," said Emily, popping her head out of Rachel's pocket. "I'm sure we'll find it if we keep looking."

The girls walked around the store, searching through the toys. They still didn't see any sign of the magic emerald.

"There's a green glow over there!" Emily said suddenly. "What is it?"

The girls rushed over to take a look.

But they were disappointed to find that the green light was coming from a computer game.

"I really don't think the emerald is

anywhere down here," said Rachel, shaking her head.

Kirsty glanced upward. "What about the next floor up?" she suggested.

The girls and Emily took the elevator up to the next floor. It was much quieter there. There were hardly any customers around, and the only salesclerk in sight was busy with some paperwork behind the counter.

"My emerald must be here somewhere," Emily whispered as the girls walked out of the elevator. "It's not far away. I can feel it!"

Kirsty blinked. Was that a green sparkle she'd just spotted, or was she imagining things? No, there it was again. "I see something!" she said excitedly. "Over there, in the stuffed animal section."

The girls and Emily hurried over to take a closer look. There were hundreds of stuffed animals. Rachel and Kirsty gazed around at the cuddly cats, dogs,

cows, penguins, zebras, and other creatures. There was even a big golden lion, with a shaggy bronze mane.

"Look," Kirsty said, pointing at a furry black cat. It sat at the very top of a pile of stuffed animals, and it had long, silky fur. But Rachel saw that it also had almond-shaped green eyes that glittered in the light.

"Could one of the cat's eyes be your

emerald, Emily?" asked Rachel, looking
up at the toy.

"Let me see," Emily replied. She
fluttered out of Rachel's pocket and flew
up to the cat, looking closely at its eyes.
After a moment, she let out a tiny squeal
of delight, and pointed to the cat's right
eye. "This is my
emerald!" she
cried.

Kirsty and
Rachel beamed
at each other.

"Kirsty, could
you get the cat
down, please?"
Emily called. "It's
too heavy for me to
pick up."

Kirsty nodded and stretched up toward the cat. If she stood on her tiptoes, she thought she would just be able to reach it.

Vrrrroooom!

Kirsty glanced up when she heard the growl of an engine overhead. As she did, she saw that Rachel and Emily were also trying to figure out where the noise was coming from.

Suddenly, the girls spotted a large silver toy plane flying straight toward them.

The pilot wore flying goggles, gloves, and a long, white scarf. But Kirsty saw that his skin was green. One of Jack Frost's goblins was flying the plane!

Kirsty turned back to the magic

emerald, determined to grab it before the goblin arrived. But, just as she stretched out her hand for the toy cat, the plane swooped toward her. As it zoomed past, the goblin reached out with a gloved hand and snatched the cat right out of Kirsty's fingers!

Goblin Getaway

"Ha, ha, ha!" the goblin cackled gleefully. "The magic emerald is mine!"

"Come back!" Emily shouted as Kirsty and Rachel glanced at each other in dismay. "Give me my emerald!"

The goblin stuck his tongue out at her. "You can't catch me!" he sneered, and

bent over the controls. The plane began to turn.

"He's getting away!" Rachel gasped.

Bravely, Emily flew up to the plane and tried to pull the toy cat away from the goblin. He quickly let go of the plane's controls and gave her a shove. The plane dipped and swerved but the goblin soon regained control. Poor Emily tumbled through the air. Her wings flapped wildly as she tried to recover her balance. Luckily, she landed gently on the pile of stuffed animals below.

Rachel turned to Kirsty. "Quick!" she cried. "You go make sure Emily is OK, and I'll try to stop the goblin from getting away."

Kirsty nodded. "Emily!" she called as she rushed to help the little fairy. "Are you all right?"

"I'm fine!" Emily panted, struggling to stand on the trunk of a cuddly pink elephant. "But please don't let that goblin escape with my emerald!"

Rachel looked around desperately for a way to stop the goblin in his tracks. His plane was heading toward the elevator and if he made it inside, Rachel thought they might never get the emerald back.

Suddenly, she spotted a huge bunch of helium balloons tied to one of the displays in the goblin's path. She raced over and untied the knot as quickly as she could. Just as the goblin flew overhead, Rachel let go of the balloons. They immediately soared upward, surrounding the plane on all sides.

"Hey, what's going on?" Rachel heard the goblin splutter. "I can't see anything!"

Rachel looked up. The goblin was trying to swat the balloons away, but to do that he had to let go of the controls. The plane dipped forward and nose-dived.

"Help!" the goblin roared. He dropped the stuffed cat and covered his eyes with both hands. "I'm going to crash!"

The plane and the black cat both crash-landed in a pile of teddy bears and disappeared. Rachel, Kirsty, and Emily rushed over. Just then, the goblin began to climb out of the heap of toys, muttering under his breath.

"He dropped the emerald," Emily whispered to the girls. "Let's find it and get out of here."

Kirsty and Rachel began searching through the pile of stuffed animals. The

goblin glared at them and dived back into the heap of toys himself. He threw stuffed animals here and there as he burrowed out of sight.

"We have to find the emerald before he does," Kirsty said.

"Too late!" the goblin declared, as he crawled out from the bottom of the pile of toys. "You won't catch me now — and you won't get this back, either!" Then he waved the stuffed cat with the emerald eye at the girls, stuck out his tongue, and ran away.

Catch That Goblin!

"Catch him!" Emily cried. "He still has my emerald!"

Rachel and Kirsty ran after the goblin, with Emily flying alongside them. Luckily, there weren't any other customers around to see the chase. But the goblin was very tricky. He dodged back and forth, disappearing behind displays. He always managed to stay one step ahead of the girls.

Kirsty slowed down and looked around.

"Where did he go now?" she asked. The goblin was nowhere to be seen.

"He was here a minute ago," Rachel said, confused. "He couldn't have just disappeared."

"There he is!" Emily shouted, pointing with her sparkly wand.

The girls turned and saw the goblin running toward the stairs as fast as he could. The toy cat bobbed up and down in his arms.

"Don't let him get away!" Rachel gasped, sprinting after the goblin.

The sudden sound of footsteps coming up the stairs made the goblin skid to a stop. Realizing that the stairs were blocked, he frantically looked around for another way to escape. Then he ducked behind some shelves stacked with toy cars and trucks.

The girls and Emily followed. They raced down one aisle just in time to see the goblin turn the corner into the next.

"I think we're catching up," said Kirsty. "Keep going!"

Rachel and Kirsty dashed around the corner and almost tripped.

The goblin was pulling boxes of toys off the shelves and throwing them in the girls' path!

"Wait a minute, girls!" Emily called as the goblin ran off again, cackling with glee. With an expert wave of her wand, Emily scattered fairy dust over the boxes. Immediately, they floated up into the air and neatly stacked themselves back on the shelves.

"Why don't we split up?" Rachel

whispered to Kirsty and Emily. "Then maybe we can trap him."

"Good idea," Kirsty agreed.

At the end of the aisle, Kirsty and Emily went left, and Rachel went right. The goblin had disappeared again. But as Rachel ran between the shelves of toys, she saw him dash across the aisle, right in front of her.

"Got you!" she panted, reaching out to grab him by the shoulder.

But the goblin was too quick for her. He snatched a blue skateboard from a nearby shelf, flung it to the floor, and jumped on. Rachel's fingers clutched at thin air as the goblin rolled across the polished floor.

"You almost had him, Rachel!" Emily shouted, flying over to her.

"Look!" Kirsty gasped, rushing to join her friends. "He's heading for the elevator!"

The elevator doors stood open, waiting for passengers to enter. The skateboard was zooming right toward them! The goblin glanced back at the girls with a smug smile, waving the toy cat triumphantly.

"Oh, no, we'll never catch him now!" wailed Emily.

But Kirsty wasn't going to give up yet. She looked at the toys on the shelves around her, searching for something, anything, that might stop the goblin. Her gaze fell on a stack of brightly painted boomerangs. "Emily, can you use your magic to help me?" she asked, grabbing one from the top of the pile.

Emily nodded and lifted her wand. Kirsty aimed the boomerang at the toy cat in the goblin's hand, and threw it. The boomerang whistled through the air,

but as it got closer to the goblin, it started to drift off course. Rachel bit her lip. It looked like the goblin was going to get away with the emerald after

all, no matter how hard they tried to stop him!

But Emily waved her wand, and a cloud of sparkling fairy dust shot after the boomerang. As soon as the fairy magic touched the toy, the boomerang swerved back on course. It flew straight toward the goblin like an arrow.

The friends watched as the boomerang spun through the air and knocked the toy cat right out of the goblin's hand!

The cat fell to the floor, but the skateboard kept going. The goblin let out a howl. He had lost the magic emerald!

Going Up

"Pesky fairy magic!" the goblin shouted. But there was nothing he could do. The skateboard was zooming along too fast for him to jump off. He glanced over his shoulder just as Kirsty and Rachel ran forward and picked up the toy cat.

"Give that back!" yelled the goblin as

the skateboard headed
toward the elevator.
"You must be joking!"
Rachel laughed.
"Shouldn't you watch
where you're going?"
called Kirsty.
The skateboard
whizzed through the
open doors of the elevator and crashed
into the back wall. The goblin fell on the
floor in a heap. He staggered to his feet,
unhurt, but he looked very
angry. He made a rush
for the elevator doors,
but they slammed shut.
He was trapped inside.
Ting! The elevator
began to move upward.

"Good-bye, goblin!" Emily called.

Kirsty and Rachel laughed, and they could hear a muffled roar of rage from inside the elevator.

"Girls, you've done it again," Emily cried, fluttering down to sit on Kirsty's shoulder. "How can I ever thank you?"

"We're just glad we got your emerald back," replied Kirsty, holding up the stuffed black cat. The beautiful magic emerald winked and sparkled at them.

"Sorry, kitty," Emily said, smiling at the toy cat, "but I need my emerald more than you do!" She raised her wand and a shower of green sparkles floated down over the black cat. The magic emerald fell gently into Kirsty's hand, and a new green eye appeared in its place.

"And now it's back to Fairyland for you," Emily added, touching her wand to the jewel. "Queen Titania and King Oberon will be very happy to see you!"

A fountain of sparkling green fairy dust shot up from the

jewel. The emerald
vanished from
Kirsty's hand.

"Rachel, we'd
better go down and
meet your dad,"
Kirsty said, looking at
her watch.

"I think we'll use the stairs!" Rachel
agreed, laughing.

"Thank you for your help, girls," Emily
said in her pretty voice.
"Every jewel you find
brings us one step closer
to returning the jewels'
magic to Fairyland." She
waved her wand. "Good-
bye, and good luck!" Then
she disappeared in a flash
of fairy dust.

Rachel and Kirsty grinned at each other and hurried downstairs.

Rachel's dad was waiting by the store's main entrance, carrying lots of shopping bags. "Ah, there you are, girls," he said with a grin. "Will you give me a hand with these?" He handed each of them a bag.

"Lucky Mark!" said Rachel, taking a peek inside. "He's going to get lots of presents for his birthday."

Her dad looked embarrassed. "Well, some of these things are for me, actually," he said. "I'm thinking of putting a toy train track in the attic."

Rachel laughed. "That sounds like a great idea, Dad."

"That was quite an adventure!" Kirsty

whispered to Rachel as they followed
Mr. Walker out of the store.

Rachel nodded. Then she grinned and
gestured toward her dad, who was
marching happily down the street with
his bags, eagerly explaining
his plans for the train
track in the attic.
"From the sound
of it, our next
adventure is going
to involve trains,
not fairies!" she said,
laughing. Somehow,
both girls knew that
wasn't true. They'd surely see their fairy
friends again soon!

The Jewel Fairies

India, Scarlett, and Emily all have
their jewels again. Now it's time for
Rachel and Kirsty to help

Chloe the
Topaz Fairy!

Goblins in Disguise

"There's a cool costume store!" Kirsty Tate said, pointing at one of the stores on Cherrywell's busy main street.

"Fun!" Rachel Walker replied happily. "Let's go pick out costumes for Isabel's Halloween party before the bus comes."

"OK," Kirsty agreed. She was staying at Rachel's house for the week, and the girls had just gone bowling with some of Rachel's friends from school. One of them, Isabel, had invited everyone to a Halloween party over the weekend. "What do you want to dress up as?" Kirsty asked Rachel.

"Something magical, of course!" Rachel replied with a grin.

Kirsty smiled back. She and Rachel loved magic. It was because they shared an amazing secret: They were friends with the fairies.

Their magical adventures had started one summer. The girls had helped the fairies stop Jack Frost from taking the color out of Fairyland. Since then, the Fairy King and Queen had asked for their help again and again. In fact,

Rachel and Kirsty were right in the middle of another fairy adventure. Jack Frost was causing trouble again!

This time, he'd stolen seven sparkling jewels from Queen Titania's crown. The jewels were very special because they controlled important fairy powers, like the ability to fly, or to give children in the human world sweet dreams. Every year, in a special celebration, the fairies recharged their wands with the jewels' magic. This year's ceremony was just around the corner. If the jewels weren't found by then, the fairies would run out of their special magic completely. The girls had to help track down the jewels!